CHICKENFEED

Based on the true story of the 'chicken farm murder', which took place at Blackness, Crowborough, East Sussex in December 1924.

Norman Thorne was found guilty of the murder of Elsie Cameron, but even at the time of his execution there were doubts about his guilt.

Still swearing his innocence, Norman Thorne was hanged on 22 April 1925.

Bestselling author Minette Walters brings a thrilling story to life in this gripping new novel.

CHICKENFEED

Minette Walters

BBC LARGE PRINT

First published in 2006 by
Pan Books
This Large Print edition published
2006 by BBC Audiobooks by
arrangement with
Macmillan

ISBN 1 4056 2184 2
ISBN 13: 978 1 405 62184 7

British Library Cataloguing in Publication Data available

Printed and bound in Great Britain by
Antony Rowe Ltd., Chippenham, Wiltshire

For my good friend Paul

Chickenfeed is based on the true story of the 'Chicken Farm Murder', which took place in Blackness Road, Crowborough, East Sussex, in December 1924.

CHAPTER ONE

Kensal Rise Methodist Church, north London—winter 1920

The skies were dark with ice-filled clouds the day Elsie Cameron first spoke to Norman Thorne. Perhaps Elsie should have taken the gloom as an omen of what was to come. But could any girl predict that a man she met in church would hack her to pieces four years later in a place called Blackness Road?

Outside, the wind and sleet beat against the Gothic spire of the Kensal Rise church. Inside, the flock huddled in their coats and listened to the preacher. He thundered against the demon of drink, which stole a person's moral sense. Cursed would be the man who hit out in temper. Or the woman who had sex before marriage.

1

Elsie Cameron, a small, plain 22-two-year-old with chewed fingernails and thick glasses, barely listened. She had heard it all before. It was a message of grinding despair to a lonely girl who suffered from depression. Elsie wanted to be loved. But the only love on offer in the chapel was God's, and His love came with conditions.

Her gaze slid sideways towards the young man who sat with his father and stepmother in a nearby pew. Each time Elsie saw him her heart beat a little faster. He was four years younger than she was—eighteen—but he was handsome and he always smiled if he caught her eye. His name was Norman Thorne and he worked as a mechanic at Fiat Motors in Wembley.

Norman's real mother had died when he was eight. At sixteen, he'd joined the Royal Naval Air Force to serve in the Great War. The war had ended three weeks after he arrived in Belgium and he never saw any fighting. But that didn't matter to Elsie. Any lad who stood up for his country was a hero.

She worried about the age difference because she had a fear of being teased. Would people call her a cradle-snatcher if she persuaded him to walk out with her? But his work as a mechanic had filled him out. No one would guess he was only eighteen. Elsie bit nervously at her fingernails as she tried to think of a way to speak to him.

Her mother had taught her that only 'loose' women made the first move. Let the man come to you, she had said. But it hadn't worked. Elsie's brother and sister had no trouble finding girls and boys to 'walk out' with. But not Elsie. Elsie scared would-be husbands away. She was too intense, too swamping, too desperate.

She feared the things she wanted, and wanted the things she feared.

She had nightmares about being left on the shelf—unwanted and unloved—but she couldn't bring herself to flirt the way other girls did. The perfect man would be content to worship her until he put a ring on her finger. And only afterwards would anything of *that* sort happen.

There was a stubborn streak in Elsie's nature that blamed others for her problems. It wasn't her fault that she was plain. It was her *parents'* fault. And it wasn't her fault that she lacked friends. Only a fool would trust people who gossiped behind her back.

Elsie worked as a typist in a small firm in the City, but her colleagues had long since grown tired of her mood swings. They called her 'difficult' and grumbled about her mistakes. She resented them for it. She resented her boss, who took her to task for failing to do her job properly.

Once in a while—in the depths of despair—she wondered if her co-workers were right. Was she difficult? More often, she blamed them for making her unhappy. If people were nice to her, she would be nice back. But why should *she* have to be nice first?

It's on such little things that life and death turn.

Would either have died if Norman hadn't smiled?

* * *

As the congregation filed out of church, Norman Thorne was a pace or two ahead of Elsie. Deliberately, she trod on the back of his heel while pretending to search through her bag. His startled face turned towards her.

She gave a squeak of dismay. 'Whoops!' she exclaimed, clutching at his sleeve.

Norman put out his hand to steady

her. 'Are you all right?'

Elsie nodded. 'I'm ever so sorry.'

'Don't worry about it.' He prepared to move on.

'I know who you are,' she said in a rush. 'Norman Thorne. I'm Elsie Cameron. We live quite close. My mum says you were in the war. That makes you a hero.'

Norman gave a shy smile. 'Not really.'

'*I* think so.'

The boy was flattered. And why not? He was young and no girl had ever looked at him this way before. Raised by a strict father, Norman neither drank nor smoked. He helped with the local Scouts, taught in the Sunday School and was involved in all kinds of chapel work.

His smile widened to one of welcome. 'Nice to meet you, Elsie.'

*   *   *

Norman's father wasn't pleased

when his son told him he had a girl.

'You're too young for such nonsense,' Mr Thorne said. 'You should put your energies into working.'

'I'm not planning to marry her, Dad.'

'Then watch how you treat her, lad. We don't want any shotgun weddings in this family.'

Nor was Elsie's mother pleased. 'He's still a boy, dear. You'd be better off with someone older.'

'He doesn't look eighteen.'

'Maybe not, Elsie . . . but he'll make you unhappy in the long run. He'll grow bored and leave you for someone else. Boys of that age always do.'

Mrs Cameron was bent over the kitchen sink, washing clothes. Her arms were deep in suds and Elsie stared at her stooped back with loathing. 'Why do you always have to ruin everything for me?' she asked.

'I don't mean to,' her mother said

with a sigh, 'but Dad and I both feel—' She broke off abruptly. She was too tired for arguments that day, and Elsie never took her advice anyway.

She had lost heart over the girl. There were no grey areas in Elsie's life. Love must be total. Support tireless. Fault-finding zero. Mild criticism, designed to help her, led to tantrums . . . or worse, threats of suicide. Elsie could go for weeks without speaking to either of her parents. Other times she fawned on them.

Conflict played a part in all her relationships. At home and at work. She could like a person one day and hate them the next. But she never understood why that turned people away. 'It's not fair,' she would say, bursting into tears. 'Why is everyone so *beastly* to me?'

Neither of her parents could see a happy ending for her. Mrs Cameron prayed she'd meet an older man who would put up with her moods. Mr Cameron said no such man existed now. If he ever had, he'd died in the war.

The war had killed so many men. It meant a generation of young women would not find husbands. For every Norman Thorne, there were five young girls begging to be noticed. And Mrs Cameron knew Elsie well enough to know that she was too needy to hold Norman's interest for long.

But, like her daughter's co-workers, she'd had enough of the petulant mood swings. 'Do as you please,' she said, drawing a pillowcase from the water and thumping it against the wooden washboard. 'Just don't come running to me when Norman Thorne lets you down.'

CHAPTER TWO

North London—summer 1921

Norman scuffed his feet along the pavement. He'd been given his cards by Fiat and was living on ten shillings (50p) a week dole money. 'Everyone's been laid off,' he told Elsie. 'It's happening all over. Dad says there's three million out of work and it's going to get worse.'

Elsie had to walk fast to keep up with his longer legs. 'What will you do?'

'I don't know.'

'You'll have to do something, pet. You can't live on the dole for ever.'

(She meant: 'If you don't find another job soon it'll be ages before we can marry.' But as usual Norman dodged the issue.)

'We were lied to,' he complained instead. 'Us lads who went away to war were told we'd come home to "a land fit for heroes". Remember that? They promised us jobs and money—' he took a swipe at a bush as he passed—'and we haven't got bloody either.'

Elsie let the 'bloody' go. Now wasn't the time to take him to task for cursing. She felt like saying she was more upset than he was. Things had been going well while he was earning. So much so that her hints about marriage had brought a smile to his face. Then he lost his job and everything changed.

There could be no talk of weddings while he was out of work. Wives and children cost money. A man should never make promises he couldn't keep. There was more to marriage than kissing. Hardship and poverty led to anger and hate.

These weren't messages that Elsie wanted to hear. Her romantic streak said love could overcome all problems. What did it matter if they were poor as long as they had each other? She knew her feelings for Norman were stronger than his for her. She called him her 'lovey', her 'pet', her 'treasure', but he only ever called her 'Elsie' or 'Else'.

She tucked her hand through his arm and put on her brightest smile. 'You're always telling me there's money in chickens. Why don't you start a chicken farm?'

'Where?' He sounded annoyed, as if he found her idea foolish. But he didn't push her away.

'Not in London. Somewhere outside. Sussex or Surrey maybe. Land's cheaper away from the city.'

He slowed to a halt. 'How would I pay for it?'

'You could ask your dad for a loan. You said he's been careful all these years. You never know. He might give you the money instead of making you wait till he's dead. He's got no one else to leave it to.'

'Do you reckon?'

'I don't see why not. Raising chickens is better than living on the dole.'

It was amazing how quickly his depression lifted. 'You could be right, Else. He said he'd give me a hand if I needed it.'

'There you are then.'

He gave her fingers a quick squeeze. 'We wouldn't see so much of each other. Sussex is a fair lick from Kensal Rise.'

'We'll manage,' she said. 'We'll write every day. It'll make our love stronger.'

*   *   *

Mr Thorne surprised Norman by the speed with which he stumped up £100 for the project. Elsie said it was because he had faith in his son. But Norman thought it had more to do with parting him from Elsie. Mr Thorne was a little too eager to see his boy move to Sussex. Perhaps he hoped that out of sight would mean out of mind.

'The change will do you good,' he said cheerfully. 'It's time you met new people and spread your wings. You're stuck in a rut here, lad.'

Sometimes Norman felt that, too. He was fond of Elsie. He even wondered if he was in love with her when she was in a good mood. But he could never predict when that would be. It got him down. There were days when she was happy, and other days when she wasn't. But it was always him who had to match his mood to hers. Never the other way round.

She called her ups and downs her 'nerves'. 'I worry about things, pet. It makes me jumpy. Mum says it'll wear off when I have a family. I can't be fretting for myself when I have children to look after.'

Norman doubted that. Surely a baby would give her more to worry about? But he didn't say so. Elsie was easier to get on with when she was making plans. She took it for granted that her future would include him.

Once or twice, he tried to suggest differently. 'I'm not the only bloke in the world, Else. Maybe you'll find someone better.'

'How can I? You're my own sweet darling.'

'Maybe *I'll* find someone better,' Norman teased, not completely in jest.

She put him through hell when he said such things. An older man might have used the sulks as an excuse to end the affair. But not a church-going boy of nineteen who was both flattered and trapped by Elsie's devotion.

Which may explain why the idea of a chicken farm outside London was as welcome to Norman as it was to his father. He hoped a breathing space would help him make up his mind.

He bought a field off Blackness Road in Crowborough, Sussex, and took it over on August 22nd, 1921. In the hope of blessing the project from the start, he named the plot Wesley Poultry Farm. (John Wesley was the founder of the Methodist Church.)

Norman lodged locally. During the day he built chicken sheds and runs. The weather was warm in September and the work was hard. His only transport was his bicycle and he was careful what he spent.

After the purchase of land, he had to buy timber and wire, while keeping enough in reserve for chickens to stock the farm. It meant he spent most of his time alone and never treated himself to a night out.

Of course he missed Elsie. She wrote to him every day so that he wouldn't forget her. 'My own darling

Norman . . .' 'Oh, my treasure, how I adore you . . .' 'Do you think of me as much as I think of you, pet . . . ?' 'Does absence make your heart grow fonder of your little lovey . . . ?'

It did. Every Friday evening he cycled the fifty miles to Kensal Rise to spend the weekend with her. But the round trip was tiring, and he warned her that he wouldn't be able to do it once the poultry arrived.

'I can't abandon them, Else. They'll need to be fed and watered Saturdays and Sundays, same as during the week.'

She became tearful, so he told her he was planning to build a hut to live in. 'It won't be much,' he said. 'Maybe twelve feet by eight feet, but there's a well for water and I can make a bed along one wall. I'll cook on an oil stove and light candles when it gets dark.'

Elsie said it sounded romantic.

Norman shook his head. 'It's the way the lads lived in the trenches,' he told her. 'Hard and rough . . . but it'll be cheaper than paying for a room every night. I'll add to it as things get better and one day it'll be a proper house.'

She was already thinking ahead. 'I can visit at weekends.'

'It's not built yet.'

'I'll come down by train and walk from the station.'

'You won't be able to stay overnight, Elsie. It'll look bad.'

'I know.' She gave his arm a teasing punch. 'Silly boy! I'll sleep in lodgings and spend the days with you. We'll have fun, pet. I'll do the cooking while you look after the chickens. We can pretend we're married.'

It did seem romantic when she put it like that. And Norman *was* lonely. Sussex folk were wary of strangers and the new friends his father had promised had never appeared. So far, his only reward for 'spreading his wings' was hard work. And hard work was joyless when there was no one to share it with.

In any case, he was a healthy young man. He still had strong chapel views, but the thought of being alone with a woman excited him.

*   *   *

He built his live-in shack to the same design as his hen houses. The walls were made of wood and a high pitched roof gave a feeling of space inside. Two beams, one above the other, ran across the centre to hold the structure rigid. At one end, a mattress on a platform served as a bed at night and a sofa during the day. At the other end, a small window let in some light.

He furnished the room with bits and pieces to make it more homely. A table and two chairs, an oil stove, a tin bowl for washing, and some matting on the floor. But, otherwise, it was just as he had promised Elsie.

Rough, hard living. Made worse by the cold as the days shortened and winter drew in.

He refused to let Elsie visit until the spring of 1922. 'The weather's too bad,' he wrote to her. 'It's hard to keep warm and most days I don't bother to wash. I sometimes think the chickens are better off than me. At least they can huddle together.'

He kept from her that the farm wasn't going well. Few of his hens were laying. Some were too young, some were off-lay, but most were affected by the rain. A local man warned him that the weather might stop the birds producing eggs for two months.

Norman was shocked. 'I can't afford to wait that long,' he said. 'I need something to sell. I'm living from hand to mouth as it is.'

The man shrugged. 'It was a bad time to start a poultry farm, lad. Chickens don't like the winter. Eggs are scarce now, but you'll have more than you can sell when the spring comes. You'll be lucky to cover the cost of the chickenfeed.'

'What will I live on?'

'Eggs?' the man suggested with dry humour. 'You'll come to hate the taste of them . . . but they'll keep the wolf from the door.'

CHAPTER THREE

*Wesley Poultry Farm, Blackness Road
—summer 1922*

Elsie loved Norman's little shack.
She'd never been so happy as on the
weekends that she spent at the farm.
She took a room down the road with
Mr and Mrs Cosham, and walked to
the field every day. She helped with
the feeding and the collecting of
eggs, but she wouldn't clean out the
hen houses.

'The smell makes me sick,' she told
Norman, wrinkling her nose. 'And I
can't go back to London reeking of
chicken mess.'

Norman didn't mind. He was
content to let Elsie sit and do
nothing as long as she was there.
Her joy rubbed off on him and he
began to think the project could
work after all. True, he was

producing more eggs than he could trade, but the cockerels and the broody hens were doing their jobs well. He now had plenty of young chicks to fatten and sell for the pot.

Elsie asked him how he was going to kill them.

'Break their necks,' he said.

'Dad says his mother in Scotland did it with a knife.'

'I don't want blood on the neck feathers.'

'Won't you have to pluck them, lovey? Who's going to buy a chicken that's not been plucked?'

'It's only the bodies that need doing, Else. You leave the heads and neck as they are so the butcher can hang them in his window. They don't look so good with blood on them.'

She squatted down to stare at a clutch of fluffy chicks. 'Poor little things.'

'Poor me, more like,' said Norman. 'I'll be plucking in my sleep if the business takes off. The feathers come out pretty easily if the bird's still warm, but it's hard work even so.'

'There'll be a lot of feathers, pet. What will you do with them?'

'I don't know,' he said, looking around the field. 'Burn them maybe. It'll make the place stink for a while but at least I'll be rid of them.'

He had more of a problem with soiled straw from the chicken sheds. He was rotting it down to sell as compost, but the process took time. Meanwhile, the growing heaps made the farm look even more run-down and tatty than it was. At first, Elsie didn't seem to notice. But after a few weeks she began to nag him about it.

'No one's going to buy your eggs if they've seen where they come from. They'll *expect* them to be bad. You need to paint the sheds. Make them look clean.'

'I can't afford to,' he said crossly. 'Paint costs money.'

'Ask your dad for more.'

'He's given me enough already.'

When her nagging became too much, he suggested *she* give him the money to buy paint. 'You say you want us to be wed, Elsie, but it won't happen if the farm fails. I know you've got savings. It won't break the bank to lend me a few quid, will it?'

'My dad will have my hide if I lend money to a man I'm not engaged to,' she said coyly. 'You'll have to put a ring on my finger first, pet.'

'And what will I buy it with? Do you know a jeweller who'll trade diamonds for poultry?'

*   *   *

But in spite of the odd argument about money and marriage, the summer and autumn passed happily enough. September and October were warm, and Elsie came down to Sussex almost every weekend. On Saturdays she and Norman lazed by a fire outside the hut when their tasks were over. On Sunday mornings they walked to the Methodist chapel in the centre of town before returning home to a meal made by Elsie.

She became expert at finding different ways to cook chicken. As often as not, the bird was an old one that needed boiling with carrots and onions. But for treats Norman would kill a young cockerel that could be fried in bacon lard from the local pig farm. It was more like camping than keeping proper house, but, as Elsie was fond of saying, 'It's like being on holiday.'

Norman's father had told him once that holidays were the worst time to fall in love. 'People act differently when they're away from home, son. You can't judge a lass by the way she is at the seaside.'

Norman wondered about that every time Elsie talked of marriage. Which was the real Elsie Cameron? The intense, nervy one who lived with her parents in London and hated her job? Or the carefree one who visited him in Sussex and played at being a wife? He knew she thought about sex almost as often as he did. Sometimes they came close to doing it.

He would pull her to him, clasping her buttocks and thrusting his hard penis against the folds of her skirt. There was always a second or two before she giggled and pushed him away.

'Naughty boy!' she'd say, wiggling her ring finger under his nose. 'You'll have to get down on your knees and propose to me, Norman. Promise to make me Mrs Thorne and I might think about it.'

'As soon as I make ends meet.'

'And when's that going to be?'

'I don't know. I'm doing my best.'

'That's all you ever say. If you loved me as much as I love you, you'd sweep me in your arms and propose anyway. I don't mind living in a hut.'

'You would if it was every day, Elsie. It's no holiday, believe me. If I can't get a butcher to take my birds, I have to go house to house to sell the flaming things. And no one pays full price . . . not when they see how desperate I am to be rid of them. A dead hen doesn't last long.'

There was no point bringing them home. The only place to hang dead birds was from the beam in his shed and they rotted quickly in the heat. On the two or three times that he'd tried it, he'd ended up burying the corpses in the field. No one wanted poultry that wasn't fresh. Worse, the smell of death attracted foxes and rats.

There were no easy answers to his money problems. He'd been foolish to start the project without learning more about farming. But there was no going back now. He kept telling himself it would come right in the end. He'd been taught that God takes care of those who take care of themselves. And that hard work wins its own reward. But worry gnawed at his gut all the time.

What if it wasn't true? What if God was teaching him a lesson in humility? How could he explain the waste of £100 to his father? How could he explain to Elsie that he might *never* be in a position to marry her?

He was always at his lowest in the hours before dawn. He lay awake, seeing himself in a trap of his own making. If he hadn't met Elsie . . . if he hadn't asked his father for money . . . if Elsie had been younger and less desperate to get married . . .

* * *

They became engaged on Christmas Day, 1922. Norman left the feeding of his birds to Mr Cosham and cycled back to London for the holiday. He told his father he was doing well enough to propose to Elsie Cameron.

Mr Thorne frowned at him. 'Are you sure, son? The last I heard you were living in a wooden hut. Is that still the case?'

'Yes.'

'Are you expecting a wife to live in it with you?'

'We're just getting engaged, Dad. The wedding won't be for a while yet, and by then I'll have found a place to rent.'

'Mm. Whose idea was it? Yours or Miss Cameron's?'

A stubborn look came over Norman's face. 'Mine.'

Mr Thorne didn't believe him. 'Will it make a difference if I refuse to give you my blessing? I quite see why Miss Cameron wants a husband—she's nearly twenty-five—but you're only twenty, lad. Much too young to start a family.'

'We aren't planning to have children straight away.'

'*You* might not be, boy, but I'm sure Miss Cameron is.'

Norman gritted his teeth. 'I'm not a boy any more, Dad, and her name's Elsie. I wish you could see her the way I do. She's sweet and kind and only wants what's best for me.'

'So do I, Norman.'

'It doesn't seem like it sometimes.'

Mr Thorne eyed him for a moment. 'Has Elsie given you a hundred pounds?'

'No.'

'Then don't accuse me of not caring.'

'I'm not,' said his son unhappily, 'but life isn't just about money, Dad.'

Mr Thorne shook his head. 'It is when you sign up for something you can't afford. There's no time for love when the bailiffs come knocking on your door.'

*   *   *

How different it was in the Cameron household. Elsie's father clapped Norman on the back and told him he was a grand fellow. 'Our girl's always wanted to be wed. She had one of her turns when her brother and sister both got engaged this year. But all's well that ends well, eh? We're glad to have you as a son.'

Mrs Cameron hugged him. 'You're a good boy, Norman. I knew you'd offer sooner or later. Our Elsie's that keen to start a family.'

Norman gave a sheepish smile. 'It'll be a while yet, Mrs Cameron. We need to find a place to live first.'

Elsie tucked her hand through his arm and stretched out her finger so that the firelight flashed on her ring. 'Not that long, pet. If you can give this to your girl, you can find a little house for her, can't you?'

Norman thought guiltily of the five pounds he'd borrowed from a moneylender to purchase the ring. 'Maybe next year.'

He was talking about twelve months hence, 1924, but the Camerons assumed he meant 1923. Elsie's brother and sister planned to wed that year, and it seemed fitting that she should, too. For the whole of Christmas Day, the chat was of nothing but bridal gowns and babies.

It was this that prompted Norman to bury his head in the sand. It was easier to agree than keep pointing out that he couldn't afford a wife and family just yet. He even became a little alarmed at how keen Mr and Mrs Cameron were to be rid of their daughter.

'She'll settle down once she's away from London,' Mrs Cameron said. 'It's the noise and the crowds that make her depressed. Try not to keep her waiting too long, Norman.'

Mr Cameron took him aside after lunch. 'Elsie gets bees in her bonnet . . . but you know that already. My advice is not to cross her. She's better when she has her own way.'

'I'll do my best, sir.'

'Good man. If you can see your way to tying the knot before her brother and sister do, you'll make her the happiest girl on earth.'

Norman knew that wasn't possible but he didn't say so. In the naive way of a twenty-year-old, he hoped the issue would go away. He thought he could stall forever as long as a date wasn't fixed.

No one could force a bloke to marry before he was ready.

86 Clifford Gardens
Kensal Rise
London

January 30th, 1923

My own darling Norman,
The worst has happened. Mr Hanley sacked me today, so your little Elsie has no job any more. He was that beastly, lovey. He said he was letting me go for the sake of the others. They've been telling lies about me again, and all because they can't bear to see me happy. They're jealous of my ring and jealous that I'm engaged. I really hate them.

Dad says I must look for another position but I won't need to if we can marry soon. Please say we can. I can't wait to be your wife, pet. I could find work as a typist in town and come home to the hut every night. We'll manage fine if I promise not to have babies for a year or two.

Oh, my darling, I love you so much. Please, please say yes.

Your own true sweetheart,

Elsie xxx

February 3rd, 1923

My dear Elsie,

I'm sorry you've lost your job but I think your father's right. You must look for another post in London. The hut's no place to live and a wife can't promise not to have babies. They happen whether you like it or not.

It's so cold at the moment that the hens' drinking water turns to ice every night. I have to sleep in my overcoat so that I don't freeze too. You wouldn't like it at all. And no one will employ a typist who can't wash herself or her clothes properly.

Patience is a virtue, Else. If we wed now we won't be as happy as if we wait. For that reason I'm sure it's better to delay.

Here's hoping you find a new job soon.

Your loving,

Norman

CHAPTER FOUR

Wesley Poultry Farm, Blackness Road
—summer 1923

Norman was coming to dread Elsie's weekend visits. Her happiness of the previous year had given way to bouts of anger and depression. She nagged him about everything. His refusal to name a day. His lack of money. Her endless misery, which she said was his fault.

Suddenly, she was unable to hold down a job. After working for the same firm for nine years, she had now been given her cards three times in five months. That, too, she blamed on Norman.

'They keep asking when I'm going to be wed and I can't tell them,' she said. 'They laugh at me behind my back.'

'I'm sure they don't, Else.

Everyone knows you have to save a bit before you can get hitched. There's loads of lads and lasses in the same boat as us.'

She stamped her foot. 'They *do* mock me . . . and I hate them for it. I can't work in a place where people give me nasty looks all the time.'

'Are you sure it's not you who starts it? If you glare at someone, they'll glare back. Stands to reason.'

But it was better not to say such things. As Mr Cameron had remarked, his daughter was happier when she had her own way. And 'having her own way' meant that Norman must agree with whatever she said. Nothing in life was Elsie's fault. If things went wrong for her, it was other people who should take the blame.

Sometimes Norman believed it. He felt guilty about raising her hopes then dashing them again. But if he hadn't proposed, she'd have been even more unhappy. A ring was proof that he loved her. It was also permission to touch her body.

Was this one of the reasons why he had begun to dread her visits? It was no longer a case of thrusting against her skirt. When she was in the mood, she let him take her clothes off and feel her naked skin. But that was as far as he was allowed to go. Showing he could control his urges was yet more proof that he loved her.

'I'm keeping myself for our wedding night, pet. A wife must be pure in body and mind when her husband enters her for the first time. You can do all sorts of other things but you can't put *that* in my body. *That* would be wrong.'

He dreamt about her when she wasn't there, and became angry when she was. 'You're a cock-teaser,' he would growl every time she pushed him away. 'You can't get a chap worked up then tell him to take a cold bath. I've got rubbers. Why can't we use them?'

'They're vulgar.'

'Who cares?'

'I don't want to talk about it.'

'All right, we won't use rubbers. I've promised to marry you so what are you scared of? I'm not going to let you down.'

'You have so far,' she would say huffily, stepping into her dress and pulling it up. 'If you fixed a date, it might be different, but I'm not giving myself to you for a cheap ring.'

'That's not what you said last summer. Last summer you said you'd think about it if I promised to make you Mrs Thorne.'

'Then make me Mrs Thorne.'

'What's the point? You'll just come up with another excuse. How do I know you'll ever do it, Else?'

'I want a baby, don't I?'

'And what happens when you have it? I sometimes think all you want is a new pet to moon over.'

These were sterile arguments that

went nowhere and only served to make them angry with each other. Both were sexually frustrated. Norman tried to deal with it by working harder. Elsie swung between moods of dark depression and moods of starry-eyed romance which she put into her love letters from London.

Oh, my dearest Darling . . . our romance is like a fairy tale and it will end with 'They lived happily ever after' . . . How I adore you, my treasure . . . you mean everything to me. I know we can manage in your little hut . . . and Elsie promises to love you always . . . Oh, my Darling, you cannot realize what you mean to me . . . I dream of the day we are together. For ever and ever, your own true sweetheart, Elsie.

Norman didn't know what to make of such letters. It seemed to him that, safely back in London, she reinvented herself as a princess in a fairy story. She forgot the hardship of the farm and saw it instead as a place of beauty. But how would he ever make her happy when the reality—mud, smell and debt—was so different?

The ups and downs of the relationship were taking their toll on Norman. More so, his never-ending money worries. Try as he might, he could not balance his books.

He was up against farmers on long-established contracts, and there was no demand for Wesley chickens and eggs. Had he planned the project better, he would have toured the area and counted the number of poultry farms. Or the number of houses that kept hens in their gardens. As it was, he'd bought the field on Blackness Road blindly.

He ran up debts with the chickenfeed producers. Then borrowed to pay them off. He told himself it was money well spent if it produced a profit in the end. All he needed was one good deal with a butcher for a regular supply of birds every week.

But his father's words haunted him. 'There's no time for love when the bailiffs come knocking on your door.'

*   *   *

As 1923 moved on towards Christmas, Elsie became more and more desperate. She'd been out of work for months, and her brother and sister had married and left her alone with her parents. Now Mr and Mrs Cameron were on Norman's back as well. They were as single-minded as their daughter. When was he going to make an honest woman of Elsie?

They might just as well have said: 'When are you going to take Elsie off our hands?' For that's how

Norman saw it. The more he avoided fixing a date, the harder Elsie's parents pressed him.

'You're breaking our girl's heart,' said Mr Cameron coldly on Christmas Day. 'May I remind you that it's now twelve months since you put a ring on her finger.'

'I know that, sir.' Norman took a deep breath to calm himself. 'But as I've explained several times I'm not in a position to marry at the moment. I need—'

Mr Cameron broke in. 'Why did you make a promise if you weren't prepared to keep it?'

I wasn't given a choice . . . Elsie forced me into it . . . I should have listened to my father . . . 'I thought the farm would come good this year.'

'And it hasn't?'

'It's only a matter of months, sir. If you could persuade Elsie to wait a little bit longer—'

'It's not my duty to persuade Elsie of anything,' Mr Cameron snapped.

'As I see it, my only duty is to remind you that you are legally bound to marry her . . . or be taken to court for breach of promise.'

A sullen expression settled on Norman's face. 'It was Elsie who wanted the ring. I was happy as we were. In any case, I haven't said I'm not willing to go through with it. I'm just asking for a little more time.'

'Which Elsie doesn't have, Norman. She'll be twenty-six in April.'

'She doesn't look it.'

'That's not the point though, is it? She feels life is passing her by. Her brother and sister are wed now.' Mr Cameron sighed. 'She says people laugh at her because she's on the shelf.'

Norman felt a twinge of pity for the man. He knew how difficult Elsie could be when she thought she was being mocked. But his pity was short lived because he blamed both Mr and Mrs Cameron for the way

Elsie was. If they hadn't spoilt her by giving way to her every mood, she wouldn't have thrown so many tantrums.

Yet the truth was he did the same himself. What else could a bloke do when his girl sulked and wept and said she was going to kill herself?

*   *   *

His own father was quick to notice his waning interest. 'You're home early,' he said, glancing at his watch on Christmas afternoon when Norman joined him in the front parlour. 'Not spending the evening with Elsie?'

'No.' Norman took a chair beside the fire. 'I need an early night. I have to cycle back tomorrow.'

'I thought you were staying longer.'

'Changed my mind.'

Mr Thorne eyed him for a moment. 'Have you and Elsie fallen out?'

'Not really.'

'Then what's the problem?'

'The usual. I can't afford to get married yet.'

A short silence fell between them.

'Is that the real reason you're putting the wedding off?' Mr Thorne asked then.

'What other reason would there be?'

'You're not in love with her any more.' He leaned forward to look at his son. 'If so, it would be kinder to be honest with her now . . . Give her a chance to find someone else.'

'She doesn't want anyone else, Dad. She's mad about me. Says she'll kill herself if I ever let her down. She has these black moods when she thinks the whole world's against her.' He dropped his hands between his knees and picked at some fluff on the carpet. 'Mr Cameron says he'll sue me for breach of promise if I don't marry her.'

Mr Thorne smiled slightly. 'I wouldn't let that scare you. It's an idle threat. No one takes a man to court unless there's money to be made out of him. And you don't have any.'

'I don't want to treat her badly, Dad. I'm still fond of her.'

'I'm sure you are, son. But it would be cruel to marry her . . . then spend the rest of your life wishing you hadn't.'

*   *   *

The idea that it would be kinder to let Elsie down gently took root in Norman's mind. He told her not to visit because of the winter cold and wrote fewer letters to her. Those he sent were cool and formal, and contained no expressions of love. He hoped she'd take the hint and give up of her own accord.

She didn't.

As his ardour cooled, Elsie's grew.

Her replies were full of passion—'I adore you . . . I worship you . . . I can't wait for the spring . . .' It was as if she thought the power of her feelings could scorch through the page into Norman's heart. How could any man fail to respond to a woman who loved him so deeply?

As often as not, Norman left the letters unopened. Just the sight of her handwriting on the envelope set his teeth on edge. He was unable to deal with so much emotion. He felt swamped and oppressed by the false picture Elsie painted of him.

He was a failed chicken farmer with mounting debts who found his fiancée tiresome. So why did she keep calling him her 'clever darling husband' and herself 'his true little wife'?

*　　　*　　　*

As soon as the weather improved, she came down to the farm for a weekend. He tried to tell her that he wanted the relationship to end. But she became hysterical, stamping her feet and hissing abuse.

'I don't *want* to talk. Do you think I'm stupid? Do you think I don't know what's going on?'

Norman shook his head guiltily. 'What do you mean?'

'Look at the sheets,' she spat. 'You've had other women in them.' She pulled the bedclothes off and kicked them against the wall. 'They're *dirty*. *You're* dirty.' Her thin body quivered with anger. 'You've been doing things on our special place. It's *hateful* . . . *disgusting*.'

He stared at her open-mouthed. 'You're crazy! I don't know any other women . . . not to kiss and cuddle, anyway.'

'What about *prostitutes*?' she screamed. 'You're wasting your money on *sluts*, Norman. I *know* you are! That's why you never have any money.'

'You need your head seeing to, Elsie,' he said in disgust.

She burst into a storm of tears and flung herself against his chest. 'I'm sorry . . . I'm sorry, pet. You don't know what it's like being away from you. I get so depressed. I get so *jealous*.'

He gave her an awkward hug. 'There's nothing to be jealous about.'

'But I don't know that,' she said, wrapping her thin arms round his waist. 'I keep thinking of you doing to other girls what you do to me. It's nice, darling. I *like* it.' She pulled him against her. 'You like it, too. *See*.'

She tried to guide his hand towards her breast, but he pulled away sharply as if she'd given him an electric shock. 'Don't,' he said harshly.

'Why not?'

'It's not right.'

Her eyes glittered angrily behind

her glasses. 'You were happy to do it last year. You can't mess with me then pretend it didn't happen, Norman. I'm not some cheap tart you can throw over when you get bored. I'm the woman you're going to marry.'

He headed for the door. 'I have to clean the chicken sheds,' he muttered. 'We'll talk later.'

Norman threw himself into work as a way to avoid contact. Elsie watched listlessly from the shack doorway. He couldn't decide what to do. Tell her outright that it was over? Or keep hoping that she would take the hint herself? Surely even Elsie—despite her strangeness —must see there was nothing to be gained by marrying a man who didn't love her?

*   *   *

But when the evening came, she behaved as if nothing had happened.

The bed was re-made, and Norman was her 'own dear darling' again. It was as if she had spent the whole day working out how to win back his favour. No angry looks. No stamping. No touching. Just healthy cooking and lots of light laugher . . . plus an endless stream of fond words.

In an odd sort of way it made Norman feel more abused than if she had forced herself on him. For it suggested that he was shallow and uncaring. Did she really believe that all he thought about was his stomach? And that food should be served with smiles and silly endearments?

By the time he walked her to the station on Sunday afternoon, he was close to strangling her. Why couldn't she see how much she repulsed him? More than anything he *hated* the feel of her coarse, chewed fingertips against his skin.

CHAPTER FIVE

Crowborough—summer 1924

Norman met Bessie Coldicott at a local dance that Whitsun. It was shortly after the weekend with Elsie. Bessie was everything Elsie wasn't. She was young. She was pretty. She was warm and understanding. And she enjoyed flirting. Best of all, she accepted Norman for what he was. A young man who was struggling to make a living in difficult times.

He loved the way she made no demands on him. With no fear of being left on the shelf, she was content to chatter about anything that didn't include wedding bells. Suddenly Norman could be the person he wanted to be. A bit of a lad. A bit of a joker.

It was a rebirth. Instead of the morose silences that had begun to mark his relationship with Elsie, he could be witty and funny with Bessie. They started walking out together within a week of the dance.

'Am I your first girl?' she asked him one day.

'No.'

'What were the others like?'

'Not a patch on you. The first one looked like a horse.' He grinned. 'The second one looked like a horse's arse.'

Bessie danced away from him. 'I don't believe you. I bet they were pretty and I bet you've had more than two. A bloke can have his pick these days.'

'I was a slow starter . . . but I'm catching up now.' He ran after her and caught her round the waist. 'Like this.' He planted a kiss on her full, soft lips.

Her eyes flashed with mischief. 'Don't go getting ideas, Norman Thorne. I've plenty of other admirers and there's some I like just as well as you.'

He knew it. All men found Bessie attractive. It was part of her appeal for him. The chase. The thrill of trying to win her. If other men had looked at Elsie in the way they looked at Bessie, he might have prized her more. But Elsie had never turned a head in her life.

*   *   *

Each time one of Elsie's letters arrived, Norman felt twinges of guilt about keeping her dangling. But like all cheats he put his own happiness first. On the two or three weekends that Elsie came to the farm during the summer, he managed to jolly her through them without too many rows. Her moods had less impact when he knew he could laugh with Bessie after she was gone.

His hardest task was keeping Elsie at bay in the shack. She was at him all the time, rubbing against him and urging him to undress her the way he used to. She told him she'd changed.

'I'm not afraid to have sex any more, pet,' she coaxed. 'It's natural when two people love each other.'

'What if you get pregnant?'

'You can use a rubber if you want.'

'I don't have them any more,' he lied. 'I threw them away. In any case, it's too dangerous, Else. Your dad'll give you hell if you end up with a baby out of wedlock.'

'I don't care, lovey. I want to show you how much you mean to me. And how can I do that unless I give myself to you?' Tears welled in her eyes. 'Please let's do it, Norman. You need to know what a good wife I'll be.'

He was canny enough to recognize that this wasn't her real reason for wanting sex. He began to see their relationship like a game of chess. Each of them was trying to force the other into a corner. Norman wanted

Elsie to realize she had no future with him. While Elsie wanted to bind Norman to her by getting pregnant.

*   *   *

In the dark hours of the night, Norman often tried to convince himself that he should marry Elsie. 'Better the devil you know than the devil you don't,' he'd say out loud.

He'd shared his life with her for four years. She knew more about him than any person on earth. There were even times when the thought of her not being there scared him. Perhaps he'd grow tired of Bessie, too.

Sometimes he wondered if he cared for women at all. His chickens gave him more affection than people did. It still upset him to break their necks and remove their pretty plumage.

He loved the way they ran when he

called to them. Necks stretched out and legs pumping. The young ones scampered so fast they fell over his feet as he walked towards them. He had to tread carefully. Some were tame enough to be stroked, others skittered away with nervous cheeps.

He had one cockerel who was a fighter. A Welsummer with blue-black tail feathers and a magnificent red comb. Norman called him Satan because of the evil that lurked in his beady eyes. If a cockerel in the next-door run strayed too close, Satan leapt at the wire and tried to attack him. He guarded his own hens jealously. Norman admired him for it.

He also admired Satan's appetite for sex, which meant few of his hens produced unfertilized eggs. This was in contrast to his Buff Orpington and Leghorn cockerels, whose milder natures made them lazy.

Which wasn't to say that Norman liked Satan. He treated him as warily as a snake after the bird attacked him from behind one time. Satan drove his sharp spurs into the back of Norman's leg and the wound hurt for days.

'I don't know why you don't kill him,' said Elsie.

'What for?'

'Teach him a lesson.'

'What's he going to learn when he's dead? And what good would it do me? Only a madman would kill his best cockerel.'

'Then teach the others a lesson.'

Norman looked at her with irritation. 'They're chickens, Elsie. Their brains are about *this* big.' He made a tiny gap between his thumb and forefinger. 'They learn where their food is and they learn to lay their eggs in the nesting boxes. But that's *it*.'

'There's no need to get snappy with me. I was only trying to help.'

'Yes, well . . . it's a stupid idea. It was my mistake anyway. I got him riled. It makes him jealous when his hens eat out of my hand.'

'His brain can't be *that* small then,' she said acidly. 'Isn't jealousy what *humans* feel?'

Norman's irritation grew. 'How would I know?' he asked unkindly. 'I've never had anything to feel jealous about.'

＊　　　＊　　　＊

He was lying, of course. He was jealous of any man who could bring a smile to Bessie Coldicott's face. She was a dressmaker in Crowborough and he took to hanging around outside the shop where she worked.

She teased him about it. 'How come you go down my street so often? The nearest butcher's two roads away.'

'It's a short cut.'

'Fibber!' She tapped him lightly on the wrist. 'You'll get me in trouble if you do it too often. Mrs Smith's a nice lady but she doesn't like men peering through the window. It upsets the clients.'

'I just want to say hello sometimes.'

She laughed. 'But not when I'm working, Norman. I like my job and I don't want to lose it. You can meet me at the back when I finish of an evening. Then walk me home afterwards.'

*   *   *

As the summer passed, he spent more and more time with her. He asked her repeatedly to visit the farm but she always refused. 'You live on your own, Norman. What would people say?'

'Who's going to see you? It's in the middle of nowhere.'

'Someone will. Bored old ladies peep through their curtains to spy on their neighbours. Everyone talks in a place like this.'

He wondered if she knew about Elsie. 'What do they say?'

'That you had a girl visit a few times. Is that true?'

He'd always known it would come out in the end. He took a deep breath. 'Yes, but there was nothing wrong about it, Bessie. She never stayed in the shack. It was all above board and proper.'

'Who is she?'

'Someone I know from London. I was keen on her once but not any more. The trouble is—' He broke off. 'She's a bit of a loony. Acts weird all the time . . . shouting and yelling one minute, crying the next. She keeps being given the sack because of it.'

Bessie pulled a face. 'There's a woman like that in our street. She bursts into tears if anyone speaks to her. Dad says it's because she lost two sons in the war, but Mum says she was born weird. She used to do it before they died.'

'Elsie's always been strange.'

'Is that her name?'

Norman nodded. 'Elsie Cameron. It was mostly her parents' idea that she came to visit. I reckon they hoped I'd marry her and take her off their hands. She's a lot older than me and they're fed up with looking after her.'

'That's horrible.'

Yes, thought Norman. It *was* horrible. Why should he be expected to make Mr and Mrs Cameron's life easier by marrying their mad daughter? *He* hadn't given birth to her. *He* hadn't spoilt her.

He reached for Bessie's hand. 'Don't worry, pet. It's not going to happen. I've loads of plans for the future . . . and none of them includes Elsie.'

'What about me? Am I in your plans?'

'Maybe.'

She gave his fingers a sharp pinch. 'Then don't call me "pet", Norman.

I'm not a fluffy chick to be kissed and stroked when you're in the mood. I'm me—and I don't belong to anyone.'

CHAPTER SIX

Wesley Poultry Farm, Blackness Road
—autumn 1924

Bessie came to tea at the beginning of September. She gave Norman twenty-four hours' notice and he spent the night and morning cleaning the shack. He couldn't believe how filthy it was. The floor was covered in chicken shit from his boots, and dust lay everywhere.

Appalled at the state of his sheets, he went into town and bought new ones. It left him short of money but he didn't think Bessie would sit on a bed that stank of sweat and grime. He folded the dirty sheets and hid them in an empty nesting box. He planned to swap them back before Elsie's next visit in case she guessed that another woman had visited.

His hard work paid off. Bessie was

impressed by the hut. 'It's quite cosy. How long have you been living here?'

'Two years.'

'Don't you get cold?'

'I do in the winter.'

She looked at the beam above her head where he stored his hats. 'That's neat. Where do you keep your clothes?'

'Behind here.' He lifted a curtain that was nailed to one wall. 'They're hung on pegs and this keeps the dust off them.'

'Neat,' she said again. 'What's in here?' She pointed to a small chest of drawers.

Norman's heart skipped a beat. *Elsie's love letters.* He should have hidden them along with the sheets. 'Razors . . . nail scissors . . . stuff that men use.'

She sat on the edge of the bed. 'It's better than I thought it would be. I was expecting something tatty.'

'Why?'

'Because you call it a shack. I thought it'd be built out of tin . . . or bits of old iron.' She patted the mattress. 'If you'd told me it was like this, I might have come sooner.'

He couldn't tell if she was giving him a come-on. Because of Elsie's moods he found women's signals confusing. Was Bessie inviting him to sit on the bed with her? Was she inviting him to go further? Or was it a test to see how much of a gentleman he was?

He bent to light the oil stove beneath the kettle. 'Where would you like your tea?' he asked.

'Outside,' she said with a smile. 'It's warm in the sunshine.' She pushed herself upright and walked to the door. 'We'll have it inside when the days turn colder.'

*   *   *

After that, Norman's life moved out of his control. Bessie started visiting the shack every night after work. And with none of Elsie's rigid views about rubbers and wedding bells, it wasn't long before they were having sex. The contrast between her softly welcoming arms and Elsie's cold, stiff fear could not have been greater.

How could he *ever* have fallen for Elsie?

*   *   *

He tried to gear himself up to tell her the truth. He wrote letters that he never sent. He even went to London at the start of October to say the words to her face. 'It's over, Elsie. I don't love you any more. There's someone else.'

He couldn't do it. She clung to him like a limpet, smiling for no reason. When he accused her of being drunk, she laughed.

'No, silly,' she said fondly. 'The doctor's put me on tablets for

71

my nerves.'

'What kind of tablets?'

She pulled a bottle from her bag. 'I don't know but they're making me better. I've stopped fretting about things so much.'

Norman read the label. 'What the heck are "sedatives", Else?'

'I don't know,' she said again. 'But I'm quite well now. We can get married whenever you like.'

'That's not—'

'We'll talk about it when I come down at the end of the month,' she said happily. 'It's all planned. I've already written to Mr and Mrs Cosham to book a room. We'll have such fun, pet.'

'But—' He stopped.

'But what, pet?'

'It'll be cold,' he said lamely.

*　　　　*　　　　*

Norman told Bessie it was his father who was coming to stay. 'He wants to see for himself how the farm's going,' he lied. 'I owe it to him, Bess. He gave me the money to get started.'

'So why don't you want me to meet him?'

'I do . . . just not yet. I've told him I'm working every hour God gave to get the business off the ground.'

'Are you ashamed of me, Norman?'

'Course not. But what's he going to think if he sees you here? He'll know I can't keep my hands off you.'

Bessie rolled on to her side to look at him. 'That's true. You're worse than Satan.'

Norman grinned. 'Except Satan does it with all the hens . . . and I only do it with one.'

She touched a finger to his lips. 'You'd better not be lying, Norman. I'll leave you if I ever find you with someone else.'

'You won't,' he said. 'You're the only girl for me, Bessie.' He wrapped his arms around her and pulled her

73

close. But over her shoulder he stared unhappily at the curtain hiding his clothes.

Elsie had stitched it for him the first time she came to the farm.

*   *   *

He cleaned the hut to remove all trace of Bessie. Strands of blonde hair. The smell of her perfume. One of her combs. He rescued the dirty sheets from the nesting box, then had to wash them to remove the smell of chickens. They ended up a uniform grey but gave no other clues that they'd been off the bed for seven weeks.

The tidiness of the shack was the first thing Elsie noticed. 'Did you do this for me?' she asked. She looked pleased.

'I wanted it to look nice for you, Else. It was a bit mucky the last time you came.'

'It didn't matter. I know how hard

you have to work, lovey. I'll keep it spick and span when I'm living here all the time.'

He changed the subject abruptly. 'How are your parents?'

'The same.' She frowned. 'Mrs Cosham said she was surprised to see me. That's a bit strange, don't you think? I booked the room ages ago.'

Norman turned away to put the kettle on the stove.

'She asked me if we were still engaged. Why would she say that, pet?'

He gave an attempt at a shrug. 'I don't know. Maybe she's wondering why you haven't been down so much this year.'

'Did you tell her about my nerves? Does she know I'm on tablets?'

'No.'

She sank on to the bed. 'That's good. I'm not going to take them any more. I hate feeling drowsy all the time.'

'But if they're making you better—'

'It's *you* that makes me better, Norman. Do you remember last summer? It was all so perfect. Just you and me in our own little house.'

'That was the year before,' he told her. 'Last year was when you got the sack . . . and your brother and sister were married.'

'We made love all the time, pet. You can't have forgotten.'

'It was only kissing and cuddling. It's not as if we had sex.'

She stared at him. 'We *did* have sex, Norman. You nearly got me pregnant.'

Norman frowned at her. 'A bloke can't *nearly* get a girl pregnant, Else. Either he does or he doesn't. In any case, we never came close to making babies. You refused to do it until after the wedding.'

'That's not true.'

He shrugged. 'You thought if I wanted sex that badly I'd marry you just to get it.'

She looked confused suddenly. 'You're lying.'

'You know I'm not,' he told her. 'I don't say I wouldn't have liked it, but—' Another shrug as he moved towards the door. 'The best summer was before we were engaged. You were pretty happy then. Do you want to make the tea? I've things to do outside.'

*　　　　*　　　　*

Elsie took all the wrong messages from Norman's efforts to keep her out of sight. She thought it was eagerness that made him collect her from the Coshams before the sun came up. And passion that kept her in the shack until well after dark. Even his sudden use of 'pet', 'lovey' and 'sweetheart' didn't rouse her suspicions.

'We can't go into town today, pet . . .' 'Stay inside, lovey. I can't bear to think of you getting your hands dirty . . .' 'It's a real holiday having you cook for me, sweetheart . . .'

Norman knew he was being cruel but he blamed Elsie for it. If she'd been halfway normal, he wouldn't have fallen out of love with her. She should have taken his hints and left long ago. How was a chap supposed to behave when he'd made a promise that he didn't want to keep?

With any other girl he could have said: 'It hasn't worked . . . No hard feelings . . . Let's go our separate ways . . .'

With Elsie it would turn into the world's greatest drama. 'You've broken my heart . . . I'm going to kill myself . . . I want to die . . .'

*   *   *

The idea had formed in his mind that the easiest way to be shot of Elsie was to marry Bessie. Once he was wed, Elsie would have to leave him alone. His plan was to write her a letter the day after the wedding.

Dear Elsie,

Yesterday I married a girl called Bessie Coldicott. She is now Mrs Thorne. I'm sorry to break it to you like this but I knew you'd create a scene if I told you before.

Yours, Norman

It was the coward's way out, but it was also the safest. If the letter made her unhappy, then her parents could jolly her out of it. And if they failed, then Norman would rather she killed herself in London than in Blackness Road.

*   *   *

'You do love me, don't you, pet?' Elsie pleaded on her last day at the farm.

'Of course.'

'Then show me.'

Norman watched with loathing as she undid her dress and let it slip from her shoulders. She was so thin that every rib stood out beneath her skin. In a pathetic attempt to make herself more appealing she took off her glasses and peered at him from eyes that couldn't see.

'Touch my breasts, pet.' She used her hands to push her flat chest into a cleavage. 'Are they pretty? Do you like them?' She dropped her right hand to her crotch. 'Do you like this, Norman? Is *this* nice?'

Oh, God!

Tears wet Elsie's lashes. 'Love me, pet. *Please*. I can't live without you. I'm so . . . *lonely*.'

With a sense of shame, Norman pulled her to him. But all he could think of was Bessie . . .

86 Clifford Gardens
Kensal Rise
London

November 16th, 1924

My dearest beloved,

The most wonderful thing! Your little Elsie is pregnant. I missed a bleed this month and the doctor says I'm expecting. It must have been when you made love to me on my last day in the shack.

I know you didn't want a baby, pet, but I promise we can manage. It means we'll have to get married as soon as possible. Dad wants it to be before Christmas. He'd rather not walk me up the aisle if I'm showing.

Oh, my darling, I am so happy. Please say you're happy too and let me know how quickly you can arrange our wedding.

Your own loving wife,

Elsie xxx xxx

Blackness Road
Crowborough
Sussex

November 18th, 1924

Dear Elsie,

Your letter shocked me. How can you be pregnant when we've never had sex? There was <u>no</u> love-making at the shack. I hugged you when you said you were lonely, but I never took my clothes off. You <u>can't</u> be expecting a baby. The doctor's wrong.

Tell your dad you've invented this story to make me marry you. If you really are pregnant then it must be some other man's baby.

Yours,

Norman

86 Clifford Gardens
Kensal Rise
London

November 20th, 1924

My own darling Norman,
I know you're upset, and I'm sorry to bring this trouble on you. But it's no good putting your head in the sand. The doctor says a girl can get pregnant from heavy petting, and you know we've done that many times. We must make the best of this, lovey, and not get cross with each other.

Dad wants us to meet so that I can prove I'm not fibbing. He says it should be in a public place so that you won't be able to shout at me. Do you remember the tea shop at Groombridge? I shall wait for you there at 3 o'clock next Monday (24th). If you don't come, Dad says he will talk to your father in the evening. The baby is making me feel sick every morning, pet, and my condition will soon be obvious to everybody. I hope you love your little Elsie enough to do the right thing by her.

Your sweetheart,

Elsie xxx xxx

CHAPTER SEVEN

Groombridge—Monday,   November 24th, 1924

The tea shop was a gloomy place. Thick lace curtains hung at the windows and dark panels lined the walls. Norman had taken Elsie there during the first summer at the farm. He'd perched her on his bicycle crosspiece and ridden the five miles to Groombridge. They'd snatched kisses as they rode through the Sussex countryside. Elsie had loved it even though her bottom had hurt for days afterwards.

Norman arrived early for the meeting but Elsie was already there. He spotted her immediately. She sat at a table in the corner, biting her nails and looking nervous. He wondered how long she'd been waiting. Hours probably. He guessed she'd been practising what to say since she wrote her letter.

She gave a little wave when she saw him. Then dropped her hand when he scowled at her. What was the point of talking to her? Did she really think he was stupid enough to accept a baby that didn't—*couldn't*—exist?

'I knew you'd come,' she said as he pulled out the chair opposite her.

'You didn't give me much choice. I don't want my father dragged into your lies.'

'I'm not lying.' She put a protective hand on her belly. 'I'm carrying your son, Norman.'

Despite himself, his eyes were drawn to what she was guarding. 'You're making it up, Elsie.'

'That's not what the doctor says.'

'How can he know? You were barely two weeks gone when you saw him. Assuming you ever went *near* a doctor. I don't believe that any more than this story you've made up about a baby.'

Elsie smiled brightly as a waitress approached the table. 'We'd like a pot of tea and some scones. My husband says I must eat for two now.'

The woman laughed. 'I'm pleased for you,' she told Norman. 'When's it due?'

'I don't know,' he said, staring at Elsie. 'When's it due, Else?'

'Next summer of course. You can't have forgotten already.' She raised her eyes to the ceiling as if to say 'Men!'

'Enjoy yourselves while you can is my advice,' the waitress said, writing their order on her pad. 'Life's never the same afterwards.' She moved away to another table.

'You're off your rocker if you think I'm going to marry you without proof,' said Norman in a low voice. 'What do you think I'm going to do when this baby never arrives? Laugh? I'll be flaming mad.'

Elsie kept the false, bright smile on her face. 'Of course the baby's going to arrive. Mum says it's a boy because he's giving me awful morning sickness. She had the same trouble with my brother.'

She tried to take one of Norman's hands but he pulled away from her.

'You might comfort me,' she said. 'It's frightening to find yourself pregnant when you don't have a husband.'

'You're not pregnant, Elsie.'

A glint of temper showed in her eyes. 'Don't keep saying that.'

'It's the truth.'

'No, it's not,' she hissed. 'The truth is you did something you wish you hadn't . . . but it's too late, Norman. Now you have to marry me whether you like it or not.' She rubbed her belly. 'Unless you want your son to be born a bastard.'

He didn't. He wanted a son he could be proud of. With Bessie. But he hesitated in the face of Elsie's anger. 'I don't see how you can be in the family way,' he said lamely. 'It doesn't make sense. How did it happen?'

This was the question she'd been waiting for. She launched into a hushed torrent of words, urging him to believe her. The doctor had told her that petting was far more dangerous than anyone realized. More babies were made by accident than were ever planned. A girl just had to touch a man and his sperm could find its way into her.

Norman shook his head in disbelief. 'How?'

'If she puts her hand on herself afterwards. Here—' She pointed towards her crotch.

Was that true?

'I undid your buttons,' she said. 'That's when it must have happened.' She lowered her voice to a sly whisper. 'I was naked, remember.'

Norman clenched his fists between

his knees and stared at the table. Despite the sex he'd had with Bessie, his only real knowledge of the birth process was egg-hatching. 'It can't be that easy, Else. Satan has to do the full thing.'

'He's a chicken, pet. Humans are different.'

Were they?

He wished he could ask Bessie. Even his father. As the waitress brought their tea and scones, he listened to Elsie prattle on about how they'd be a proper family by next summer. But her tone had a fake jollity, as if she was more intent on convincing strangers than convincing Norman.

Later, when he walked her to the station, she ordered him to arrange the wedding as soon as possible. 'I'll tell Mum and Dad it'll happen before Christmas.'

He refused her offer of a kiss. 'You're taking a lot for granted, Elsie.'

'Why shouldn't I?' she said with a tremor of fear in her voice. 'It's *your* baby, Norman. You *have* to marry me.'

'And if I don't?'

'I'll kill myself,' she sobbed tearfully. 'And you'll be to blame.'

*   *   *

When Bessie came to the shack that evening Norman asked her if a girl could get pregnant by touching a man's 'thing' when he had his clothes on. She giggled. 'You mean like this?' she asked, feeling his penis through his trousers.

'No. Putting her hand through his fly . . . then touching her fanny afterwards.'

'Like this?' She undid his buttons and fluttered her fingers around his foreskin before reaching under her skirt.

He grabbed her round the waist and nuzzled her neck. 'I met a bloke this morning who said that's how his sister got pregnant.'

'He's lying,' said Bessie with another giggle. 'The silly cow's been at it hammer and tongs and doesn't want her parents to know.'

'That's what I thought.'

'So who is this bloke?'

'No one you know,' he said, lowering her on to the bed. 'And I wouldn't tell you anyway. If the girl wants to lie that's her business.'

'Except you'd have to be daft as a brush to believe rubbish like that. If touching was all it took . . . every girl in the world would be pregnant.'

Blackness Road
Crowborough
Sussex

November 25th, 1924

Dear Elsie,
   I have thought long and hard
about what you said yesterday
and I'm afraid I do not believe
you're pregnant. For this reason,
I shall not be arranging our
wedding this week. There are one
or two things I haven't told you.
Life has been difficult this last
year. The farm is in debt, and
someone else has been helping
me through my problems. I am
between two fires at the moment
and need time to decide what is
best to do.
   Yours,

Norman

86 Clifford Gardens
Kensal Rise
London

November 26th, 1924

My own darling Norman,
I don't understand. Of course
I'm pregnant. Why won't you
believe me? And who is this
someone else? I really do think
you owe me an explanation.
Your loving,

Elsie xxx

November 27th, 1924

Dear Elsie,

What I haven't told you is that a girl comes here late at night. It started when you gave in to your nerves again and felt that life wasn't worth living. I lost hope that we could ever be happy together. This other girl is different. She makes me laugh and keeps me going through the bad patches. I have strong feelings for her or I wouldn't have done what I've done.

I'm sorry to upset you.

Yours,

Norman

Blackness Road
Crowborough
Sussex

November 27th, 1924

Dear Dad,
I could do with some advice.
I've run into some problems with
the farm and with Elsie. Is there
any chance you could visit in the
next few days?
I'm sorry to be a nuisance.
Your loving son,

Norman

86 Clifford Gardens
Kensal Rise
London

November 28th, 1924

Dear Norman,

You've broken my heart. I never thought you could lie to me like this. I gave you myself and all my love and you have betrayed me. It's a poor thing for a man to give up on his wife just because her nerves are bad. You don't seem to care how I feel. You don't write a single word of love, yet I stood by you when you were out of work.

I expect you to finish with this other girl and marry me. Let me know what date you've fixed by return. I shall love you for ever and always in spite of

what you've done.
  Your devoted,

Elsie xxx

CHAPTER EIGHT

Blackness Road—Sunday, November 30th, 1924

Norman jumped out of his skin when Elsie smacked him on the arm. He was busy cleaning out the chicken sheds and had his back to the road. He was humming to himself and his mind was full of Bessie.

'What the hell—' he cried, ducking away from her and raising his arms to protect himself. He certainly hadn't expected to see Elsie.

She pounded at him with her fists. 'I *hate* you,' she spat. 'Who's this other girl? What's her name? Why didn't you answer my letter?'

Norman warded off the blows. He'd never seen her so mad looking. Her hair was unkempt and her face red with anger. 'I only got your letter this morning,' he fibbed.

'Liar! You'd have got it yesterday. I want my wedding, Norman. When's it going to be?' She kicked his leg. *'Tell me!'* she screamed.

Chickens scattered in alarm. 'Take it easy,' he begged. 'You're scaring the hens.'

But she wouldn't be side-tracked. *'Now,* Norman . . . tell me *now.'*

'Soon,' he said desperately, dodging another punch. 'It'll be soon.'

She dropped her fists. 'When?'

'Before Christmas.'

She examined his face to see if he was lying. 'That had better be the truth. If I find out you're lying again—' She broke off on a sob. 'How *could* you, pet? I thought I could trust you.'

'You can,' he said lamely. 'I was planning to write today. Do your parents know you're here?'

She shook her head.

'Then they'll be worried. You

should go home. I'll walk you to the station.'

'I'm not leaving,' she said stubbornly. 'I won't go back to London till I'm a married woman. Everyone's saying it's never going to happen. But it *is*. You're promised to me . . . you've *always* been promised to me.'

What could Norman say other than yes? There was no reasoning with Elsie when she was like this. He wanted to tell her to take a tablet but feared another onslaught from her fists. In this mood, anything could fuel her anger. And he had a bigger problem. He needed to be rid of her before Bessie came to the shack that evening.

So he lied. He told Elsie he loved her. That he wanted her baby. That of course the wedding was on. The other girl was history. Just a silly mistake that had happened when he was lonely.

'But you must go home now, Else.

You can't stay here till we're married. People will talk.'

'I don't care.'

'But *I* do,' he said firmly, steering her towards the gate. 'I want a wife I can be proud of . . . not one that's called a tart.'

And of course Elsie gave in. As Norman knew she would. It was her worst fear. That people would sneer at her behind her back.

But did anyone—apart from Norman and her family—even remember that Elsie Cameron existed?

*   *   *

That night Norman told Bessie the truth. He did it badly. Kept starting with: 'Do you remember when I said . . .'

Bessie took it in her stride. 'I'm not an idiot, Norman. I found Elsie's love letters weeks ago. That's what women do . . . search their men's things.'

He was more relieved than offended. 'And?'

'I asked Mrs Cosham about her. She said Elsie's got mental problems . . . and you're the poor lad who drew the short straw. Elsie couldn't care less who she marries, as long as she marries someone.'

'I liked her at the beginning, Bess.'

She propped her hip against his arm. 'You were a baby . . . chickenfeed to the first grasping woman you met. You have to be straight with her. Tell her you don't love her any more.'

'It's not that easy. She gets—' he sought for a word—'hysterical.' He sighed. 'I wish she'd just go away and leave me alone.'

'But types like that don't, Norm. She'll keep at you till you do what she wants. I knew a bloke like it once. Walked out with him a couple of times and he acted as if he owned me. Even smacked me in the face once because he reckoned I was smiling at another man.'

Norman was shocked. It was one thing for Elsie to hit him, another for a man to do it to Bessie. 'What happened?'

'My dad sorted him out. Told him he'd take his head off his shoulders if he came near me again. It worked a treat. He left town and I never saw him again. Maybe you should ask your father to do the same for you.'

'Dad's never hit a woman in his life.'

'He doesn't need to. All he has to do is make Elsie understand that you're never going to marry her. She might believe it if it comes from him.'

*   *   *

But Mr Thorne refused to do his son's dirty work. It was three days later when he came to the farm in response to Norman's letter. They

105

were inside the shack, sheltering from the wind. Norman stuttered through another explanation, then asked his father to speak to Elsie on his behalf.

Mr Thorne cast a critical eye over his son's living arrangements. 'You can't bring a wife into this,' he said.

'I know . . . but Elsie won't listen to me, Dad. She might to you, though.'

'Maybe she will, but it's a shabby way to tell her you're not going to marry her. I thought I brought you up to be more honest than that, son.'

'You did, but—'

'I'm disappointed in you, Norman. You're a Methodist with Christian values. You should never have invited her here on her own.'

'I know, but—'

'I thought you had more sense.'

'But I never *did* anything, Dad.'

'Are you sure?'

'Positive. It might have happened the way she says the first summer we were here. We got pretty close at times.' He squeezed one fist inside the other. 'She's lying. I'll eat my hat if she's even been to a doctor.'

Mr Thorne sighed. 'Then don't commit yourself to a wedding until well after Christmas. If she's telling the truth, it should be obvious by the spring. If she isn't, you can be shot of her with a good conscience.'

'But you don't know what she's like,' Norman said wretchedly. 'When she came here on Sunday, she was planning to stay until I married her. What if she tries that again?'

'Show her who's boss,' Mr Thorne said reasonably. 'Give her her marching orders. Put her on the train.'

Norman massaged his knuckles. 'You've never seen her when she's angry. She's like a mad woman . . . screaming and yelling.'

'I thought she was taking pills for her nerves.'

'Not on Sunday, she wasn't. She

kept hitting me.'

Mr Thorne frowned. 'It's a bad business, son. But I did warn you.'

Tears of despair rose in Norman's throat. 'So what do I do?' he asked gruffly. 'I don't even like her any more . . . and I sure as hell don't want to marry her.'

'Then keep delaying. There's nothing else to be done. Except pray that you're right about her not being pregnant.'

'I am right, Dad. I don't need to pray about it.'

'Then *I* will,' said Mr Thorne, standing up. 'I'm not as arrogant as you, Norman. It's God who decides when and how a child is born.'

*　　　*　　　*

'Supposing Elsie *is* in the family way?' Norman asked Bessie that evening. 'No one's going to believe it isn't mine. I'll have to marry her whether I like it or not.'

'She's not.'

'How do you know?'

'She can't even persuade you to sleep with her.'

He rested his forehead in his hands. 'She's not that ugly, Bess.'

'All right. Let's say another man *has* shown an interest. Why would she want to marry you and not him?'

'Maybe he's married already.'

Bessie gave a grunt of amusement. 'Oh, come on! Where would they have done it? In her parents' bed? In his *wife's* bed?'

'That's disgusting.'

'Well, her only other choice would have been a stand-up quickie in a back alley. Is she a prostitute?'

'Don't be stupid.'

'It's you who's being stupid, Norman. There's no *way* Elsie can be pregnant. Your Dad's right. You have to stick it out and call her bluff . . . even if she does make your life hell in the meantime . . .'

Blackness Road
Crowborough
Sussex

December 3rd, 1924

Dear Elsie,
Dad came to visit today. He's not happy about a rushed wedding and says we must wait till after Christmas. Hope you understand.
Yours,

Norman

CHAPTER NINE

Kensal Rise, north London—Friday, December 5th, 1924

The hairdresser had pinned Elsie's hair into a neat coil at the back. Now she teased the fringe into a cloud of soft curls around the girl's face. 'Going somewhere nice?' she asked, nodding towards the overnight case at Elsie's feet.

Elsie stared at herself in the mirror. She'd asked for a new style that took attention away from her glasses. Had it worked? Did it make her look pretty? 'Sussex,' she said.

'I went to Brighton once.'

'I'm having my wedding there.'

'That's nice,' the woman said. 'I suppose it's cheaper out of season. When's the big day?'

'Tomorrow.'

'Goodness! Who's the lucky chap?'

'Norman Thorne,' Elsie told her. 'He's a farmer . . . has his own house and everything.'

The woman smiled. 'And all I got was two rooms and a dustman. Where did I go wrong, eh?' She framed Elsie's face with her hands. 'How's that, dear? Will it suit?'

'Oh, yes. Norman won't recognize me.' Elsie lifted the little case on to her lap and moved aside a wash bag to find her purse. 'How much?'

'Sixpence should cover it.'

*   *   *

The hairdresser couldn't help noticing how little was in the case. A baby's frock, two pairs of shoes and the wash bag. She wondered what kind of girl would go to her new home with no knickers.

There was even less in the purse. When Elsie had paid for her new hairdo, there were only a couple of pennies and a train ticket left.

Still . . . It wasn't a hairdresser's place to question a client's word.

But, oh, my goodness! How she longed to tell the skinny little thing that her green knitted dress didn't suit her. And that chewed fingernails and the desperation behind her horn-rimmed glasses put lovers off quicker than anything.

Blackness Road
Crowborough
Sussex

Sunday, December 7th, 1924

My own darling Elsie,
   Well, where did you get to
yesterday? You said you were
coming on Saturday so I went to
the station to meet you. Did
something go wrong? Let me
know as soon as possible.
   Your ever loving,

Norman

Telegram, 10.00 a.m. Wednesday, December 10th, 1924

From: Donald Cameron, 86 Clifford Road, Kensal Rise, London

To: Norman Thorne, Wesley Poultry Farm, Crowborough

Elsie left Friday. Have heard no news. Has she arrived? Reply.

Telegram, dated 3.00 p.m. Wednesday, December 10th, 1924

From: Norman Thorne, Wesley Poultry Farm, Crowborough

To: Donald Cameron, 86 Clifford Road, Kensal Rise, London

Not here. Cannot understand. Sent letter on Sunday.

CHAPTER TEN

Blackness Road, Crowborough— Friday, December 12th, 1924

It was at times like this that PC Beck wished he was thinner. It was hard work pedalling his heavy cycle along Blackness Road. When he reached the Wesley Poultry Farm and saw the muddy state of the field, he gave up on the bike and went looking for Mr Thorne on foot.

He found him in one of the chicken sheds. 'Mr Thorne? *Norman* Thorne?'

'That's me.' Norman wiped his palms down his trousers and offered an open hand. 'Sorry about the mess. The rain's chewed up the ground. What can I do for you?'

The policeman returned the handshake. 'I'm here about Miss Elsie Cameron, sir. I believe you and she are engaged.'

'That's right. Has she had an accident or something?'

'That's what we're trying to find out. Her father reported her missing yesterday. He says she left London a week ago to come down here.'

Norman shook his head. 'I haven't seen her. She told me she was coming on Saturday . . . but she never turned up. I wrote the next day to ask what was going on but I haven't had a reply. All I've had is a telegram from her dad.'

'Do you mind telling me what you were doing last Friday, Mr Thorne?'

'Not in the least.' Norman gestured towards his shed. 'How about a cup of tea? It's warmer inside. I can give you a photograph of Elsie if it helps. I'm pretty damn worried about her, you know.'

But not worried enough to come to the police station himself, thought PC Beck sourly as he picked his way through the mud. He studied the picture of Elsie while Norman set the kettle to boil.

'Mr Cameron says she left his house on Friday afternoon,' he said, taking out his notebook. 'Do you want to give me your movements from lunchtime onwards?'

Norman's memory was surprisingly good. He recalled in great detail what he had been doing on Friday, December 5th. Shortly after lunch he had cycled to Tunbridge Wells to buy some shoes. On his return at around four o'clock he had fed his chickens and collected some milk from Mr and Mrs Cosham.

'After that I made some tea and took a nap,' he said. 'I was whacked. The round trip to Tunbridge Wells is a killer.'

'But Miss Cameron didn't come here?'

'No. I went out again a bit later . . . about a quarter to ten I should think. I'd promised to walk a couple of lady friends home from the station. Mrs Coldicott and her daughter. They spent the day in Brighton and came back on the ten o'clock train.'

'Address?'

Norman gave it to him. 'I stayed at their house about fifteen minutes and was back here for half-eleven. There was no sign of Elsie . . . but I wasn't expecting her till Saturday.'

'How do you know the Coldicotts?'

'The way I know most people round here. Mrs Coldicott buys a hen from time to time.'

'What did you do on Saturday, Mr Thorne?'

'Fed and watered the chickens then went to the station to meet Elsie. She told me she'd be coming in on the ten-fifteen. I waited around for an hour then caught the train to Tunbridge Wells.'

'Was that normal?'

'What?'

'That she stood you up?'

Norman stared at him for a

moment. 'I didn't think of it as standing up. I assumed she'd had to stay home for some reason. Do you mean was I worried?'

'If you like.'

'Why should I have been?'

PC Beck shrugged. 'No reason. What did you do in Tunbridge Wells on Saturday?'

'Nothing much. Walked around a bit, then came home again. I checked at the station in case Elsie had come on a later train, but no one had seen her. So I stopped off at the Coshams for some milk and asked if she'd booked in with them. But she hadn't.'

'Is that where she usually stayed?'

Norman nodded. 'They'd planned a party for Saturday night. I was hoping to take Elsie to it.'

'Did you go anyway?'

'No. The Coshams cancelled it because not enough people could come.'

The policeman made a note. 'What

did you do instead?'

'Went to the Coldicott house. There was a film I wanted to see at the cinema. I asked Miss Coldicott if she wanted to come with me.'

PC Beck took another glance at the photograph of Elsie. 'How old is Miss Coldicott?'

'Twenty.'

'Is she a special friend, Mr Thorne?'

'No. She just likes going to the movies.'

'And you say you wrote to Miss Cameron the next day, asking what had happened to her?'

'That's correct.'

'Do you have her letter to you, saying she'd be down on Saturday?'

'We didn't arrange it by letter. She was here the weekend before. We agreed the day and time then.'

PC Beck took the mug of tea that Norman handed to him. 'Do you have any idea what might have happened to her?'

Norman shook his head again. 'I did wonder if she nodded off on the train and ended up in Brighton. She takes pills for her nerves. They make her go to sleep in the oddest places.'

'But she wouldn't have stayed there, would she?'

Norman pulled a face. 'I don't know. She might be trying to scare us into taking notice of her. She can act pretty strange at times.'

*   *   *

PC Beck gave a report of this conversation to his inspector.

'What did you make of him?' the man asked.

'He's a young chap. Looks as if he's struggling to make ends meet. His place is more like a pigsty than a chicken farm. But he's pleasant enough and looks you in the eye when he answers questions.'

'So you think he's telling the truth?'

'I checked with Mr and Mrs Cosham and they confirmed what he said. I also visited the Coldicotts. They did the same. But I'm not sure Bessie Coldicott is quite the casual friend he claimed. She's a handsome piece and she talked about Thorne's farm as if she's a regular visitor.'

'Interesting.' The inspector steepled his fingers under his nose. 'According to Mr Cameron, his daughter was pregnant by Thorne. Is Bessie attractive enough to make the lad wish he hadn't been so careless?'

'Oh, yes,' said Beck drily. 'In terms of looks, there's no contest.'

*   *   *

Elsie's photograph appeared in the newspapers that weekend under the caption: *'Has anyone seen this woman?'*

It prompted two flower growers in Crowborough to come forward. They told the police they'd

123

passed someone matching Elsie's description at ten past five on the day she went missing. She was walking in the direction of Wesley Poultry Farm.

This time a team of officers visited Norman's farm. He was asked if he had any objections to the huts being searched. 'Of course not,' he told them. 'I want to help all I can.'

The inspector sent his men to check the chicken sheds while he went into the shack with Norman. He refused to sit down or take a cup of tea. Instead he moved about the room, pulling open drawers and examining Norman's clothes.

He asked Norman the same questions that PC Beck had asked. And received the same answers. 'You have a good memory, Mr Thorne.'

'My life's pretty boring. There's not much to remember.'

'So the last time Elsie came here was Sunday, November 30th?'

Norman nodded. 'I haven't seen her since.'

The inspector eyed him for a moment. 'And how often have you seen Miss Coldicott in that time?'

'Just once,' said Norman truthfully.

Bessie had been in the shack when a reporter came to the door. Norman hid her from view by stepping outside and closing the door behind him. But Bessie had taken fright.

'I don't want to be in the papers,' she said after the reporter had left. She was trembling.

Norman tried to comfort her.

'No,' she said, pushing him away. 'I can't see you again till this is over. I won't bring scandal on my family, Norm.' She slipped away in the dark without saying goodbye.

The inspector might have been reading Norman's mind. 'I'm told you've had reporters here, Mr Thorne.'

'I didn't invite them. They just

keep coming.'

'But you show them around and let them take photographs of you with your chickens.'

Norman gave a morose shrug. 'What else can I do? If I refuse, they'll say I have something to hide. They hang around the gate, waiting for me to come out.'

The inspector felt sorry for the lad. He had no liking for the press either. 'It's not easy. What are these stains?' he asked, pointing to the table.

'Blood and guts,' said Norman. 'It's where I pluck and pull my hens. Sometimes I joint them and take their heads off. It depends what the customer wants. There's a fair amount of mess if I do a batch at a time.'

'Where do you hang the birds?'

'From a beam in one of the empty sheds.' He looked up. 'Sometimes from this beam.'

The inspector followed his gaze. 'The one you keep your hats on?'

'Yes. I move them to make room.'

'How do you reach it?'

'Stand on a chair.'

'May I?'

Norman pushed a seat towards him. 'Be my guest.'

The inspector hoisted himself up and looked along the beam. 'It's very clean. The upper beam's dusty . . . but not this one.'

'It's harder to reach the top. If I stored anything up there, I wouldn't be able to get it down.'

'But why are there are no feathers, Mr Thorne? You seem to have done a splendid job of cleaning this place.'

'I do my best. A chap shouldn't let his standards go just because he lives alone.'

The inspector stepped down and replaced the chair under the table. 'But you don't feel the same about the outside? Your chicken runs look as if you've taken a plough to them.'

'It's the hens. They scratch for worms.'

The lad had an answer for everything, the inspector thought. He watched Norman closely as he asked his next question. 'Why was Elsie walking along Blackness Road the day she went missing, Mr Thorne?'

Norman's eyes widened slightly. 'I don't understand.'

'Two witnesses saw her at five-ten. They said she was heading here.'

'It can't have been Elsie.'

'They recognized her from the photograph you gave us.'

'Well, she never arrived,' Norman said flatly. 'I'll swear on any Bible you like that I have not seen Elsie Cameron since the end of November.'

Blackness Road

December 31st

My darling Bessie,
It's been so long since I saw you. I really hoped we could spend Christmas together. But things are getting better now. The reporters have gone and the police accept that Elsie never came here. I now wonder if she killed herself in secret somewhere. She always said she'd do it if I let her down.

She had a strange nature and not very kind parents. They forced her on me because they were bored with her moods. I should have listened to my father. But like you say, I was too young to know what I was doing.

Honour bright, darling, I have never felt for any girl as I do for

129

you. I was drawn to Elsie out of loneliness. I'm drawn to you out of love. Dearest of pals, you keep me going through the dark hours. I hope it won't be long before this nightmare is over and we can be together again.

Your own dear,

Norman

Groombridge Road
Crowborough

January 13th

Dear Norman,
   Sorry not to have replied before but we've been busy at work. I don't think we should see each other for a while. Dad doesn't want me walking out with you until the police go away. People might gossip. I'll write again when I can. Mum and Dad aren't too keen, though.
   With love,

Bessie

CHAPTER ELEVEN

Wesley Poultry Farm, Blackness Road
—January 14th, 1925

A shadow darkened the doorway of the shack. Norman looked up from Bessie's letter to see a stranger standing there. Hastily, he used the sleeve of his jumper to wipe tears from his eyes. 'Can I help you?' he asked.

'Chief Inspector Gillan of Scotland Yard, Mr Thorne. I'm here to arrest you.'

'What for?'

'Involvement in the disappearance of Miss Elsie Cameron. We have a warrant to dig up your property.'

Norman looked past him to where several policemen were leaning on spades. 'What happened to the other inspector?'

'Scotland Yard was called in a

week ago. I've been running the case since your neighbour, Mrs Annie Price, gave evidence to Sussex police. She saw Miss Cameron walk through your gate at five-fifteen on the evening of December 5th.'

Norman knew Annie Price. She was one of Bessie's despised curtain twitchers. A woman with nothing better to do in life than spy on her neighbours. 'It wasn't Elsie,' he said.

The Chief Inspector stepped into the shack. 'Then who was it, Mr Thorne?' He read Bessie's letter over Norman's shoulder. 'Miss Coldicott?'

'It wasn't anyone. I was here alone.'

Gillan put a hand under the young man's arm and hauled him to his feet. 'I'm betting Elsie's somewhere in this ploughed field, Norman. But if I'm wrong, I'll be the first to say sorry.'

*   *   *

Four hours later, Norman was asked to account for the contents of an Oxo-cube tin. Found under a pile of rubbish in his tool shed, the tin contained a broken wrist-watch, some cheap jewellery and a bracelet.

'Do these belong to Elsie Cameron?' Gillan asked him.

'Yes . . . but it's not what you think. She hid them there the last time she came.'

'Why? They aren't worth anything.'

The question threw Norman. 'I don't know,' he said. 'She didn't tell me why.'

*　　　*　　　*

At nine-thirty the next morning, Gillan showed him Elsie's overnight case. It was sodden and filthy. 'Do you recognize any of this?' he asked, removing the baby's frock, the two pairs of shoes, the wash bag and a pair of damaged spectacles.

134

Norman stared at the items.

'The case was buried near your hut. We think these are Miss Cameron's glasses. Who put them there?'

Norman didn't answer.

'If we find her body, you'll be charged with murder. Do you understand that? And the penalty for murder is to be hanged by the neck until you're dead. Is there anything you want to tell me that might save your life?'

Norman ran his tongue across dry lips. 'No,' he whispered.

*   *   *

Ten hours later, he changed his mind. At eight o'clock in the evening he asked to speak to Chief Inspector Gillan.

'I didn't kill Elsie,' he told him, 'but I know where her body is. It's under the chicken run where the Leghorns are.'

'Do you want to make a statement, Norman?'

'Yes.'

'Then I must remind you that anything you say will be taken down and may be used in evidence against you.'

Sussex Constabulary

Statement given by Norman Thorne at 8.15p.m. on January 15th, 1925

I was surprised when Elsie arrived at the farm on Friday, 5 December. It was shortly after five o'clock in the evening. She was in an angry mood. She calmed down when I gave her a cup of tea and some bread and butter. I asked her why she had come and where she planned to sleep.

She said she was going to sleep in the shack. And that she intended staying there until we were married. I told her she couldn't do that and we had a bit of a row. At seven-thirty, I went to the Coshams to see if they could put her up for the night.

They were out.

When I got back to the farm Elsie was in a bad temper. We had a row about Bessie Coldicott. Elsie cried because I'd been unfaithful. I cooked her a boiled egg to raise her spirits. She calmed down again until about nine-thirty when I told her I had to meet Bessie off the train.

Elsie tried to stop me going. She yelled at me and pulled me towards the bed. She said she wanted me to sleep with her. I refused and told her to go to bed on her own. She started sobbing. I could hear her as I went to the gate.

I walked Bessie and her mother home from the station then returned to the farm about half past eleven. The light was on in the shack. It was shining through the window. When I opened the door I saw Elsie hanging from the beam by a piece of washing-line cord. I couldn't believe it. I cut the cord and laid her on the bed. She was dead. She had her frock off and her hair was down. I put out the light and lay on the table for about an hour.

I thought about going to Dr Turle and knocking up someone to call the police. Then I realized the position I was in. There were so many people who knew I didn't want to marry Elsie. Who would believe I hadn't killed her? The only thing I could think to do was bury her body and pretend I'd never seen her.

I got out my hacksaw and sawed off her legs and head by the glow of the fire. I did that because I thought smaller pieces would be easier to bury. I put her head in a biscuit tin and wrapped the rest in newspaper. I dug holes in the chicken run nearest the gate and put Elsie into them.

Then I burnt her clothes and cleaned the shack. I was afraid to tell the truth before. Elsie always said she'd kill herself if I let her down. But I never thought she'd do it.

Signed:

Norman Thorne

CHAPTER TWELVE

Crowborough police station—January 16th,1925

Chief Inspector Gillan folded his hands on the table. 'What happened to the washing-line cord?'

'I burnt it with her clothes.'

'Why did you do that? Why did you keep her jewellery?'

Norman ground his knuckles into his eyes. 'I moved all her things on to the bed when I cut her up . . . then forgot about them. She was completely naked . . . nothing on at all.' He took a breath. 'I found her stuff when I started to clean up . . . but I was too tired to dig any more holes by then. It was simpler to throw her clothes on the fire and hide her jewellery in the tool shed.'

'You buried her suitcase.'

'I didn't want to burn the baby's

dress. It didn't seem right.'

Gillan offered him a cigarette. 'The post-mortem showed she wasn't pregnant. You were telling the truth about that at least.'

'I know.'

'But you're lying about everything else, Norman. She didn't hang herself. There were no rope marks on her neck. And there's no sign that a body ever swung from your beams. They're made of soft pine. There should be a groove where the cord bit into the wood.'

'I can only tell you what I found.'

'Then explain how her watch and glasses came to be broken.'

'Maybe she broke them herself. She was very het up.'

'Not good enough.'

'Maybe I broke them when I lay on the table. Maybe she stood on them after she took them off.' Norman dropped his head into his hands. 'She was blind as a bat . . . but she thought she looked better without them.'

'Did she?'

'No.'

Gillan ran his finger down a piece of paper in front of him. 'The body was in good condition because the weather was cold and you buried it the same night. The post-mortem found bruises on Elsie's face. Did you punch her?'

'Of course not. I never hit Elsie.'

'You had an argument with her.'

'But I didn't *hit* her, Mr Gillan. I wouldn't have told you about the row if I had. She went down like a sack of potatoes when I cut the cord. I was standing on a chair, and there was no way I could support her weight. I think her head knocked against the chest of drawers. Would that have caused bruises?'

'I don't know. I'm not an expert.' The Scotland Yard man moved his finger down a line. 'According to this, she died two hours after eating a light meal.'

Norman leaned forward eagerly. 'Then that proves I didn't kill her. She was alive when I left the shack at nine-thirty.'

'There's only your word for that.'

'Except we didn't have supper till after eight-thirty. First, I went to the Coshams and then we had a row about Bessie before I started cooking.'

'But there are no witnesses to any of this, Norman. The Coshams were out and you and Elsie were alone.'

'How would I know the Coshams were out if I didn't go there?'

Gillan shrugged. 'It was a month before you made your statement. Anyone could have told you.'

Norman wiped his palms nervously down his trousers. 'But if she didn't hang herself . . . and I didn't hit her . . . then how does the post-mortem say I killed her?'

Gillan took his time about replying. This was the one bit that troubled him. 'It says she died from shock.'

'What does that mean?'

'Her nervous system failed. Her heart stopped and she collapsed.'

Norman stared at him. 'Does that mean her nerves killed her? How could that happen? She was always giving in to them . . . but she never came close to dying before.'

'It depends what you did to her. This reports suggests you punched her several times in the face then left her to die. If you hadn't . . . if you'd stayed with her and brought her some help . . . then I wouldn't be charging you with murder.'

'But I didn't do anything, Mr Gillan. You have to believe that. It happened the way I said in my statement.'

Gillan pushed back his chair. 'Then you shouldn't have taken her head off. It's easier to see rope marks when the neck's intact.' He stood up. 'You treated that poor girl with no more respect than you show

a dead chicken. And policemen
don't like that, Norman.'

CHAPTER THIRTEEN

His Majesty's Prison, Lewes—March 3rd, 1925

As Norman's trial approached three months later, his defence team became worried about his state of mind. He was putting his faith in God and seemed unaware that the weight of the evidence was against him. Sir Bernard Spilsbury, England's most famous pathologist, had carried out the post-mortem. And Spilsbury had come down firmly in favour of murder.

The chief medical expert for the defence was Dr Robert Brontë. He had performed a second post-mortem and was willing to say he'd found rope marks on Elsie's neck. He would also argue that 'death by shock' should not result in a murder conviction. There was no evidence that Elsie's death was intended. Nor that a collapse could have been predicted.

But Dr Brontë enjoyed none of Spilsbury's fame and the jury was less likely to believe him. Spilsbury had been the crown expert witness on every famous murder trial since 1910. His word alone could swing a jury.

The defence team felt that only Norman's father could make him understand how serious his position was. To this end, Mr Thorne was given leave to speak to his son in Lewes Prison the day before the trial. He was shown to a room on the ground floor of the remand wing.

'Bearing up all right?' he asked when Norman was brought in.

They shook hands. 'Pretty much. It's good to see you, Dad.'

He looked so young, thought Mr Thorne. Just a boy still. 'Sit down, son. Your barrister, Mr Cassels, has asked me to talk to you about the trial. We're all praying for a not guilty verdict, but—' He broke off. How could he tell his only child that he might hang?

Norman reached across the table and gently stroked his father's hand. 'But the jury might believe this Spilsbury fellow?'

Mr Thorne nodded.

'Mr Cassels says they have to prove I *meant* to kill Elsie. But how can they do that if she died of shock? You can't *frighten* someone to death.'

'Spilsbury will argue that the bruises on her face show you hit her . . . and that her watch and glasses were broken during the attack. If she was in a bad way when you left her to meet Bessie, then the jury might feel you meant her to die.'

'What about the rope marks that Dr Brontë found?'

Mr Thorne sighed. 'It's only his opinion, Norman. Spilsbury will say

149

there were no rope marks.'

'But there *were*, Dad. I saw them when I cut the cord away from Elsie's neck. I just don't understand why they can't tell she died from hanging. Doesn't it show in your lungs if you can't breathe?'

'She may never have intended to kill herself. According to Dr Brontë, just drawing a noose round your neck can cause shock.'

'That's what Mr Cassels said. But I don't understand why.'

'It's something called the vagal reflex. Some people are extremely sensitive to pressure on their necks. There's a case of a woman who died within three seconds of her lover's hand caressing her throat.'

'But I found Elsie hanging, Dad. She *meant* to do it.'

'Perhaps not. Perhaps it was a little piece of drama that went wrong.'

Norman shook his head. 'I still don't understand.'

'Dr Brontë thinks she was planning to frighten you. If she had the noose ready for when you came home . . . then stood on the chair when she heard the gate open—' Mr Thorne broke off on another sigh. 'Death by vagal reflex would have caused her to fall forward. That's why you found her hanging.'

Norman stared. 'Are you saying it was an accident?'

His father nodded. 'It could have been. Which is why there were no marks on the beam. She wasn't there long enough. Not if you cut her down as soon as you found her.'

'I did,' Norman said with sudden excitement. 'Will the jury believe me? Will they believe Dr Brontë?'

'Maybe . . . if we can prove she used threats of suicide to get her own way. We can certainly prove she was no stranger to play-acting. She told everyone she was pregnant. Even bought a baby's dress to keep up the pretence.'

'I *told* you she was lying, Dad. Her parents should have put her in a hospital. She wasn't right in the head. She needed help.'

'Two of her co-workers will say that in court, but whether anyone will believe them—' Mr Thorne lapsed into a brief silence. 'You should have gone to the police when you found her, Norman. Why didn't you?'

His son's eyes grew bleak. 'Because they wouldn't have believed me. They don't believe me now.'

'They might have done. It was cutting her up that makes people think you're a murderer. Elsie deserved better, Norman.'

A shudder ran through the boy's frame.

'What made you do it?'

Tears wet Norman's lashes. 'It didn't seem so bad. She was just another dead thing. I reckon you shut down your feelings when you have to kill chickens all the time. Will the jury understand that, Dad?'

'No, son,' said Mr Thorne sadly. 'I don't think they will.'

EPILOGUE

Norman Thorne was found guilty of the murder of Elsie Cameron on March 16th, 1925. He was sentenced to death by hanging. The date of his execution was fixed for April 22nd. By strange chance, this would have been Elsie's twenty-seventh birthday had she lived.

Public concern was expressed about the verdict. There were many who felt the trial had failed to prove 'beyond reasonable doubt' that Norman had caused, or meant to cause, Elsie's death. Even Sir Arthur Conan Doyle—the creator of Sherlock Holmes—was moved to ask questions.

It came to nothing. Norman's appeal against his conviction and sentence was rejected. The night before his hanging, he wrote to his father. It was a letter full of hope.

There will be a flash and all will be finished. No, not finished, just starting for I go to God. I'll wait for you just as others are waiting for me. I am free from sin. With all my love . . .

AUTHOR'S NOTE

It interests me that Norman Thorne never confessed to killing Elsie Cameron. Not even on the gallows. To the end, he swore he found her hanging in his shack. This doesn't prove he was innocent. But for a young man who believed in God, it was a dangerous gamble to take if he was guilty. Norman knew that a sinner must repent if he wanted to go to heaven.

I believe the truth is what I've suggested in this story. Elsie planned to frighten Norman when he came home by standing on a chair with a noose round her neck. But her cry for attention went wrong. Perhaps the cold made her clumsy. Perhaps she pulled the noose too tight by accident.

In some people, the vagal or carotid reflex kills rapidly.

Compressing the nerves and arteries in the neck causes the brain to shut down and the heart to stop. This form of 'accidental' death can occur during solo sex acts when a noose is used to enhance orgasm. Victims—usually men—tend to be recorded as 'suicides' to avoid upsetting their families. However, the best-known use of reflex black-out is when Mr Spock presses his fingers to a person's neck in *Star Trek*. Even though *Star Trek* is fictional, the principle is the same.

Psychoanalysis was still in its infancy in 1924, but those who knew Elsie Cameron described her as mentally unstable. They said she was 'depressed', 'neurotic' and 'nervy'. She had a fear of being left on the shelf and thought people laughed at her. Her co-workers complained that she was 'moody' and 'difficult'.

Her problems grew during her four-year relationship with Norman. She couldn't hold down a job. She wanted to be loved in a 'fairy tale' way and was obsessed with getting married. She swung between anger and depression when she couldn't have her own way. A doctor tried to cure her condition with sedatives (probably an early form of barbiturates).

Elsie's behaviour suggests she suffered from Borderline Personality Disorder. Sufferers of BPD have low self-image and are often depressed. They can be difficult to live with. They have constant mood swings and become angry when they feel let down. They think in black and white terms, and form intense, conflict-ridden relationships. Threats of suicide are common.

Whatever happened the night Elsie died, I am sure her disturbed state of mind played a part in her death. Either her stubborn refusal to leave provoked Norman into hitting her, or she staged a 'suicide' to make him feel guilty enough to give up Bessie.

At Norman's trial, the jury was swayed by Sir Bernard Spilsbury's testimony. They decided that Elsie collapsed as the result of an attack and that Norman had intended to kill her. Yet, even if he *had* hit her, there was no evidence she was dead when he left the shack. Nor that he could have predicted she would die later from shock.

I'm more persuaded by a sentence in Norman's statement. He said he found Elsie suspended from the beam with her 'frock off and her hair down'. Yet it was a cold December night. Norman himself would have been wearing an overcoat. Why would it even occur to him to say he found Elsie hanging naked . . .

. . . unless it was true?